ROSEBUD

LUDWIG BEMELMANS

AN UMBRELLA BOOK

Alfred A. Knopf • New York

AN UMBRELLA BOOK PUBLISHED BY ALFRED A. KNOPF, INC.

Library of Congress Cataloging-in-Publication Data

Bemelmans, Ludwig, 1898 -1962
Rosebud / Bemelmans.
p.   cm.
Summary: When Rosebud the rabbit reads that, unlike the whale and the elephant,
he is regarded as a weak and silly animal, he sets out to prove he is the smartest of all.
ISBN 0-679-84913-0 (trade) — ISBN 0-679-94913-5 (lib. bdg.)
[1.Rabbits—Fiction. 2.Animals—Fiction.]   I.Title.
PZ7.B423Ro   1993   [E]—dc20   92-47046

Manufactured in the United States of America
10 9 8 7 6 5 4 3 2 1

Once upon a time there was a Rabbit
by the name of Rosebud, who was very
happy—

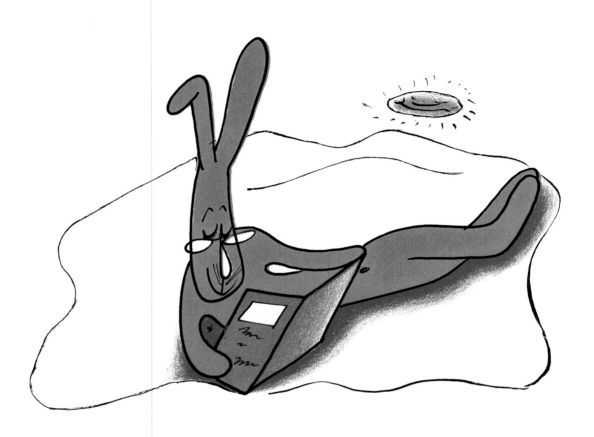

Until the day he found a book.

"The Lion," said the book, "is—

—THE KING OF THE ANIMALS. He
is intelligent, ferocious and brave. He kills
his enemies and both man and beast are
afraid of him.

"The Camel and the Dromedary are the ships of the desert. They carry heavy burdens and can go for days without a drink of water.

"The Elephant is known for his great strength, for his patience and for his wonderful memory.

"The Whale is the largest of mammals.
He swims day and night through endless
stretches of sea, swallowing tons of fish.

"The Rabbit is a small rodent who lives in burrows. He is scared, shy and hysterical. He runs and hides whenever he can. He is hunted everywhere, but in spite of that he multiplies."

After Rosebud had read this far, he closed the book with a bang, and he got madder and madder and madder, and then suddenly—he heard a noise. At first he wanted to run, but then he said to himself, I won't, I won't, I won't run—I'm going to see where this noise comes from.

So he hopped down to the sea, and there he saw a Whale. "Heavens!" he exclaimed in first surprise. And then, "Gosh, what an immense animal! What a tremendous creature!" But then he remembered the book, and he went close to the Whale and said—

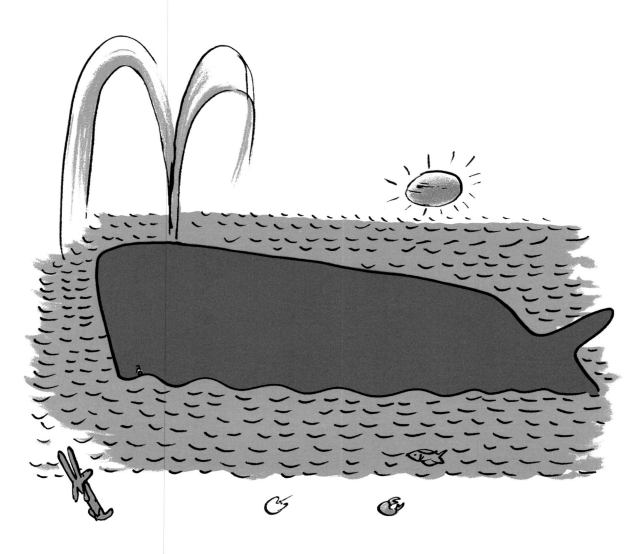

"Bah! Anyone with eyes in his head can see that you are big—but it's all just tons of fat and blubber.

"It isn't size that counts, it's muscle and sinews—I'll prove it to you.

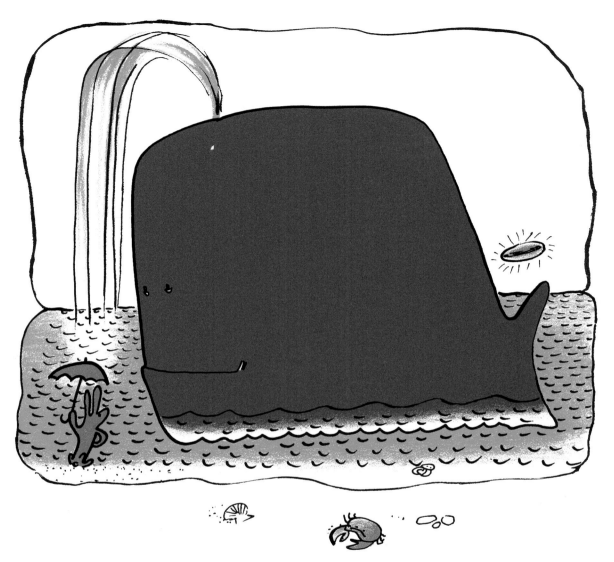

"Come back here tonight, and you'll find me waiting with a stout rope. One end of it is for you to tie around your middle—I'll take the other end and when I count to three we'll both pull.

"You'll be surprised—when you find yourself out here on the sand!"

The Whale promised to come back after
dark. He laughed so loud that the sea was
filled with ripples—and then he swam away.

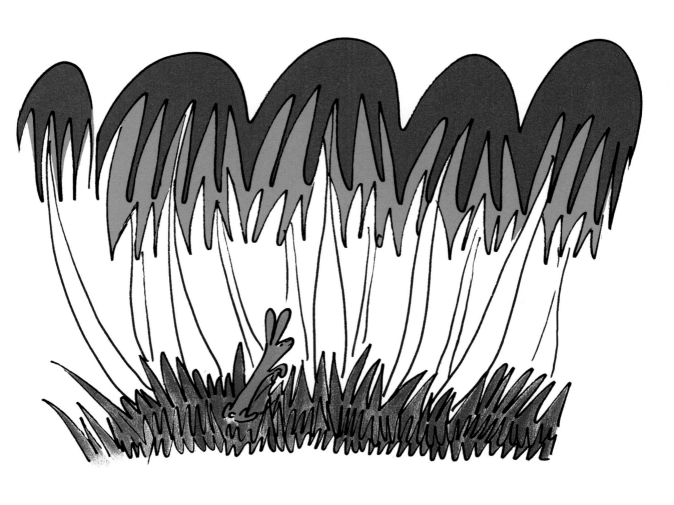

Rosebud went into the Jungle to look
for an—

ELEPHANT

"Pah! Big head, small tail. When looking
at you, Mr. Elephant, one can't fail to
observe that people with so much bulk
can't possibly be good for anything—except
being in the way.

"I suppose you know it isn't size that counts.
It's sinews and muscle that win the fight!

"Tonight, when it gets dark, I shall bring a stout rope. One end I will wind about my middle and the other I shall give to you.

"Next I shall count to three and then we'll each pull and the world will find out which one of us is the stronger."

"All right, all right," said the Elephant. "Run along now, go get your rope. I'll be waiting for you." The big bulk lay down to rest again.

As soon as the moon was in the sky,

Rosebud appeared with a long rope.

First he ran down to the beach

and gave one end to the Whale—

Then he ran back and gave the other
end to the Elephant.

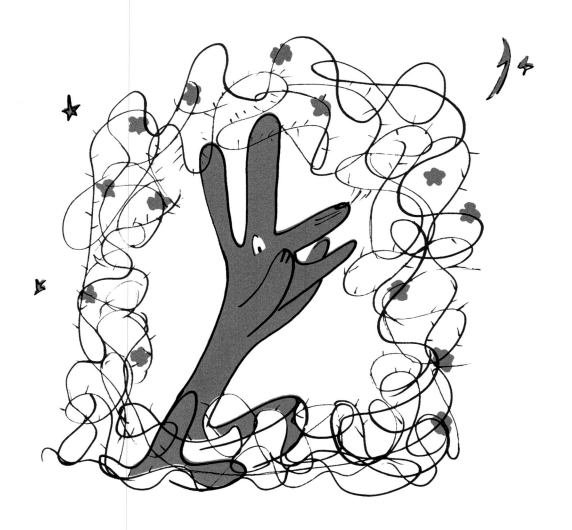

Next, he hid in a rosebush and from
there he shouted:

"ONE—TWO—THREE!"

The Elephant, who had wound the
rope twice around his middle, grunted
and puffed and sweated.

The Whale pulled with all his might
and thrashed the water into high waves
until—with a loud

SNAP—the rope parted!

The Elephant lay on his back in the grass—

while the Whale came to grief on a coral reef.

"Oh, Mr. Big, before you leave, take a look at yourself," said the Rabbit. "Take a good look, and then swim to the end of your ocean and tell your friends of this experience. And don't forget to mention my name!"

"And you," he said to the Elephant, "remember what happened just now—with your celebrated memory. Remember forever that one must never make fun of little people. Go on—run along now!"

Saddened, the Elephant and the Whale left, but
Rosebud stayed and felt better.

He started to write a magnificent book about the
strength and smartness and the great courage of rabbits.